AN UNSOUND MIND

ROLF SÖDERLIND

Copyright © 2017 by Rolf Söderlind

All rights reserved. This book or any portion thereof may not be reproduced or used in any manner whatsoever without the express written permission of the publisher except for the use of brief quotations in a book review.

Cover: Anstey's Cove at the base of Bishop's Walk in Torquay, Devon. Photo: Rolf Söderlind

Published in the United Kingdom

First Edition, 2017

ISBN (Print Edition): 978-1-9998075-1-1
ISBN (Kindle Edition): 978-1-9998075-2-8

Rolf Söderlind
Torquay, Devon

soderlind@btinternet.com

TO HEATHER

DISCLAIMER

This is a work of fiction. Names, characters, businesses, places, events and incidents are either the products of the author's imagination or used in a fictitious manner.

Break, break, break,

On thy cold gray stones, O Sea!

And I would that my tongue could utter

The thoughts that arise in me.

Extract from *In Memoriam*,
— Alfred Lord Tennyson

CHAPTER ONE

"Hurry on," Amanda told Mairi, "get your coat and hat. We only have a couple of hours." Mairi sprinted to the entrance hall to fetch her brown coat and matching hat. They were setting off from Windsor Court where both worked, Amanda as the long-serving cook, and Mairi as the newly employed house parlourmaid.

"I need to post this letter home." Mairi left an envelope on the window sill while putting on her coat.

Amanda looked at the address on the letter with a raised eyebrow, but said nothing.

"I like your coat." Mairi glanced at Amanda's blue tweed.

"Thank you." Amanda turned to Mairi with a smile so disarming it made her smile, too.

"I'll show you the sea. Cannot believe you haven't seen the sea yet."

"Aye, but I saw the sea when Mr Clifford picked me up at the railway train station yesterday," Mairi countered.

"You only caught a glimpse of it from the motor car." Amanda led the way in the morning sun past flowerbeds down the gravelled driveway of the two-storey grey stone house owned by Mr and Mrs Clifford. "Come on. I'll show you."

Mr Clifford, a tall, dapper man in his late thirties, impeccably dressed, a sartorial expert with dark hair and a pencil-thin moustache, came to the entrance and shouted, "Mrs Ackroyd, please make sure to be back in time for lunch and look after Mairi."

Amanda, a Devonshire native in her mid-twenties, turned around and smiled. "Don't worry Mr Clifford. I shall bring back Mairi safe and sound."

Mairi, a twenty-year-old Scottish lass, looked back as well and smiled. She had been impressed by Windsor Court the moment she arrived late in the afternoon on the day before. The house was up in the Torquay hills, a half hour walk from the town centre near the seaside. She had marvelled at the imposing entrance door with the brass doorbell in the middle, the parquet floors, the high ceilings, as many as twelve fire places, lead mullion windows, the gardens with their sweeping lawns, roses, raised beds for vegetables and big greenhouse. It was a world apart from her terraced home in Scotland.

"So what's it like to work for these people?" Mairi glanced at Amanda as they sauntered down the road past fields where farm hands were toiling away.

"He is a true gentleman, is Mr Clifford, even though he is strict on protocol of course. You need to put in the hours. But his wife is a different kettle of fish. She wants to find faults."

Amanda stopped and looked Mairi in the eye. "You must stand up to her or she will treat you like dirt. I stood up to her once and since then she treats me with respect. I have been a cook here for four years now. You want to stay? Put in the hours but above all stand your ground against that woman. She's been away seeing her sister in Totnes this weekend as I've told you, but you'll meet her in an hour or so. Mr Clifford has gone to fetch her."

Mairi took in the advice, feeling a sense of unease mixed with determination. "Aye. I do hope to stay here for a year or two. My father expects it of me."

They encountered the occasional motor car and horse-drawn cart on their way to Anstey's Cove. Here a narrow foot path called the Bishop's Walk took them up a steep hill with a vertiginous drop to the rocks on the waterfront below. From the top they had a fabulous view of the English Channel with the sky meeting the blue sea on the horizon.

"Cross the channel and you'll come to France and if you turn to starboard you sail into the Atlantic Ocean and, beyond it, America." Amanda threw out her arm in a dramatic gesture to the west.

Mairi found this a difficult idea to take in. She breathed in the salty smell of the sea and was fascinated by the scene before her. It was as if she could see forever. The openness of the sea reminded her remotely of the majestic view she once had enjoyed from a mountain near home overlooking the loch, having walked up the mountainside with her father and little brothers.

Then she found herself staring down at the rocks, 150 feet below her, with the waves crashing over them in a white foam. From nowhere came the thought: what a scary, lonely place to die. Feeling dizzy, she grabbed Amanda by the shoulder to steady herself.

"Are you all right?" Her friend gave her a quizzical look.

"I felt unwell looking down the hill," Mairi mumbled. "Let's move on."

Amanda nodded. "It's steep. Wouldn't want to take a tumble down them cliffs."

Amanda, a natural leader full of life and vigour, again walked ahead and Mairi was happy to follow her, mindful not to look at the cliffs below. It was true she had never witnessed the sea before coming to this exclusive seaside resort, having grown up in a coal miners' village in Lanarkshire. And here she was on a Sunday in April 1933, hundreds of miles from home about to start work as a house parlourmaid in charge of cleaning rooms and serving meals cooked by Amanda, and she would often get to eat the same food as the Cliffords, only in the kitchen, not the dining room.

Saturday's railway train journey had taken most of the day and Mairi had soon finished her sandwiches and fruit that she carried in her bag. She had had to change trains in London, which she had found stressful partly because of the trouble finding the right platform and partly because she had never seen so many people before, such a crowd. By the time the train pulled into Torquay station Mairi had been hungry and worried that nobody would come and pick her up, or maybe not recognise her. She already missed her father but told herself to be strong because she had embarked on the adventure of her young life. She was a big girl now and next year she turned twenty-one and would be allowed to vote. She wanted the family back home to be proud of her and she had written a letter to her father promptly on arrival at Windsor Court so he would know all was well.

The two young women walked down the coastal Ilsham Marine Drive past a few houses on the right-hand side, whose inhabitants enjoyed splendid sea views, and onto the Torquay waterfront where Mairi was astonished at the number of people sitting on park benches enjoying the sun or walking on pavements along the sea among trees on this lazy Sunday morning. She walked up to a tree that was of a kind she had never seen before.

"It's a palm tree." Amanda noticed her curiosity. "We have many of them here because of the warm climate."

Mairi touched the palm tree and sniffed at it. It smelled like any old tree and she wasn't that impressed after all.

But she admired two elegant middle-aged women who were in the middle of a conversation next to a lamp post. They wore fine apparel. "Everyone here in Torquay seems to be better dressed than me, but I guess that's to be expected."

Amanda inspected her. "You could do with a better coat, but they are expensive. Never mind, now let's have an ice cream."

She bought vanilla ice cream cones for both of them from a street parlour.

"Thanks, but are you sure I shouldn't pay for mine?" Mairi sampled the ice cream, which was delicious.

"Don't even think of it. As the most senior servant in the house I earn more than you do."

"Is that why Mr Clifford referred to you by your surname? I mean, I heard him call you Mrs Ackroyd. He doesn't call me Miss Craig. I don't mind, but still."

"Yes well, I am treated better because of my position in this house. I cook for them so they show respect."

"Aye, but why Mrs Ackroyd? You cannae be married. You don't wear a wedding ring."

Amanda patted her on the shoulder. "It's a courtesy title acknowledging my position in the household. You've got a lot to learn, but I will help you. Any questions? I will do my best to answer them."

They sat down on a bench next to a flower bed dotted with daffodils and crocuses. Amanda turned to Mairi. "We could go to the pictures one evening. There is also a library up the road in the town centre if you want to borrow books."

Mairi was pleasantly surprised. "I've never been to a cinema. It would be fun to go and see one of them American films I've read about in the paper. And I certainly like reading novels."

They rose and Amanda showed Mairi a post box. She took out the envelope from her pocket and slipped it into the post box with a satisfied look on her face. They then made their way to the harbour with all the wooden sail boats, including a single-mast 35-foot sloop.

"That's Mr Clifford's boat by the way. See that teak deck? Isn't it beautiful?"

Mairi was in awe. "I know nothing about boats, but it's big so it must be seaworthy. Do the Cliffords go out sailing a lot?"

Amanda shook her head. "No, Mrs Clifford gets seasick. But he sets out on day trips on the bay with business friends, mostly on Saturdays."

Mairi noticed that some of the boats were fishing vessels. The sharp stench from the lobster pots drying in the sun caught her by surprise and was almost overwhelming. Seagulls wheeled across the sky, screaming as they looked for food.

"I could do without them seagulls." Mairi grimaced.

Amanda spotted the time on the harbour clock tower. "Oh, my goodness! We'll have to hurry. Mrs Clifford is a right tartar if she catches you coming back late."

It was noon and they had been gone for about an hour and a half. Sunday lunch was served at one o'clock. They were allowed a two-hour break every day and now they started to walk up the hilly Babbacombe Road, leaving the harbour behind them and heading for Windsor Court.

Amanda turned to Mairi. "That letter to your father. I noticed in the entrance hall that you had addressed it care of the Post Office in your village. Why didn't you address it to your home?"

Mairi frowned, bit her lip and for a little while concentrated on walking up the road.

Then, in a quiet voice, she said: "Och, it's a long story. My ma and I, you see, don't get along. If she had spotted my letter first, chances are she would have thrown it on the fire and my father would never have seen it. He is dear to me."

Amanda gave her a lingering look. Mairi however did not elaborate, and they continued to walk back to the house, now in an awkward silence.

Sarah, a stout, middle-aged lady with a kind but resigned face, stood by the entrance door at Windsor Court, hoping to see Amanda and the new girl emerge from down the road. Sarah was the third servant in the house and her main duties were sewing and looking after the children, two little boys who were not yet of school age. Her surname was Collingwood, but she was always referred to by the Cliffords as Sarah. She had made preparations for Sunday lunch in Amanda's absence. She sometimes stood in for her. Pudding had been prepared beforehand and Sarah had cooked the beef in the oven. All Amanda needed to do was to boil potatoes and other vegetables while Mairi laid the table in the dining room.

"Are they running late?" Mrs Clifford, a dark-haired woman in her thirties who could look attractive were it not for that air of dissatisfaction in her face, appeared next to Sarah with her little boys. "They'd better not be."

"They should be here in the next five minutes." Sarah turned around and looked at the clock on the wall in the hall.

Mrs Clifford, followed by the boys, walked upstairs. "James and John, we need to get you properly dressed."

Suddenly, Amanda and Mairi appeared down the road and Sarah returned to the kitchen with a sigh of relief.

The kitchen was a long and narrow room at the back of the house, with the cooker at the near end to the left and cupboards, a work bench and the kitchen sink lining the walls, along with a walk-in larder and a table with chairs at the far end. This was where Amanda and Mairi had their meals while Sarah would usually eat lunch and supper with the boys in the nursery.

"Right, here is your white apron and hat." Amanda presented Mairi with a lace-edged pinny to go over her black maid's uniform and a little starched piece of decorative headgear.

Mairi went to the hall and looked herself in a mirror. She had to smile. The hat was so bonnie.

"Mairi. Lay the table now and then ring the dinner gong." Amanda sounded bossy as she usually did when she felt stressed.

The dining room had a table for six and it would always be laid for the Cliffords at both ends.

"Good luck Mairi. I'm off to the nursery." Sarah left the kitchen with food and drinks on a tray for her and the children.

This was the first time Mairi did any work in the house and she felt the pressure, biting her lip. The dining room was round the corner from the kitchen. She noticed a brass bell on the table, the far side, where the lady of the house would sit. Having laid the table, she rang the Victorian dinner gong on the floor by the wall.

Mr Clifford entered the dining room and greeted Mairi with a jovial smile. "Good afternoon Mairi. I hope you are settling in well. How do you find Torquay?"

Mairi blushed and stared at the floor. Mr Clifford had a natural confidence and ease, which stood him in good stead in his positions as a local councillor and a solicitor, a member of a law firm.

"Oh, I like Torquay a lot thanks, Sir." She found courage to look him in the eye. "Amanda, I mean Mrs Ackroyd, bought me an ice cream."

Mr Clifford smiled. "That was most kind of her. Mrs Ackroyd is obviously looking after you. I am pleased."

Mairi beamed at his encouraging words, but her heart sank at the sight of a stern-looking Mrs Clifford, who wore a black dress that matched her permed dark hair. The mistress, all pearls and pursed lips, gave the new parlourmaid a curt nod and a not-too-subtle glance over. Mairi served Mr Clifford first as instructed, then Mrs Clifford without setting a foot wrong. Relieved, she then went back to the kitchen to await further orders. Amanda was cleaning up in the kitchen, Mairi helped her and they sipped tea. Suddenly a bell rang.

"That's Mrs Clifford calling on you. Better go there now and clear the table for the dessert." Amanda beckoned for Mairi to make a move.

"What kept you?" Mrs Clifford gave Mairi an admonishing look.

Mairi was confused. "Sorry Madam, I didn't know what the bell meant at first, but Mrs Ackroyd explained it to me."

Mrs Clifford nodded. "Well, next time be quicker about it."

Her husband squirmed.

Mairi removed the plates, cutlery and glasses to the kitchen for washing up.

"Come on, give her a chance," Mr Clifford was saying as Mairi was no longer within earshot. His wife scoffed at him.

Mairi went back to the dining room to serve pudding and then sat down with Amanda to have a much-deserved Sunday roast lunch in the kitchen.

In the evening Mairi stood in front of the mirror in the bedroom she shared with Sarah in the western wing, next door to Amanda's bedroom, which was smaller but she had it all to herself by the backstairs in close proximity to the kitchen and the lavatory and wash basin on the ground floor below. There was a bathroom at the other end upstairs but it was reserved for the family.

With Sarah downstairs preparing herself to go to bed, Mairi took a moment to inspect her face. She needed a better coat, but she was fairly pleased with her looks; the thick reddish blonde hair whose locks seemed to live a life of their own, her green eyes, high cheek bones and slim figure. People always said she had a pretty smile, but she thought her lips too narrow and envied Amanda for her full mouth. One thing Mairi definitely didn't like about her own appearance was the mole in her left eyebrow. She had heard that a surgeon could easily cut away a mole, but imagined it would be an expensive operation, far beyond her means.

Continuing her comparisons, Mairi acknowledged that Amanda was taller than her, but wasn't as good-looking in her view despite those full lips, although the cook had rather a curvaceous figure, which some men might like. Mairi touched her breasts, maybe she was too slim. One day she hoped to find a handsome man she would want to marry, have children, a home of her own, financial security. Maybe that man was here in Torquay? She was eager to find out.

There was really no need for a fire now the weather was getting warmer and, anyway, Mairi shared not just the room but also the double bed with Sarah and they warmed each other with their bodies, which the nurse had told her was a blessing in winter when the coal fire in the room had died in the night and stormy weather from the Atlantic, the dreaded southwesterly wind, would hit Torquay. Sarah came to bed and they said goodnight. Mairi felt that the long walk with Amanda had done her good and she drifted off to sleep.

Eerie darkness fell over Bishop's Walk and a strong wind from southwest sent enormous waves crashing into the cliffs below. Dark silhouettes of seagulls scaled the sky like menacing shadows with piercing screams. No living soul should be out here at this hour. But Mairi Craig the new house parlourmaid at Windsor Court stood on the foot path staring down the abyss, terrified beyond belief and wanting to scream, but paralysed by fear. Not a sound came from her mouth.

Suddenly her mother, with that accusing look in her dark eyes, appeared out of nowhere. "Jump!" she hissed with rotten breath, as Mairi felt her foothold begin to loosen at the edge of the crumbling cliff face.

"What's the matter with you?" Sarah shook Mairi. "Stop tossing around. I am trying to sleep."

Mairi sat up with a start, sweat on her forehead. "I had a nightmare. Thank God it's over."

CHAPTER TWO

"Good morning Mairi." It was Monday before breakfast and Mrs Clifford, wearing a grey skirt with a black blouse and her trademark pearl necklace, was going to show her new employee the ropes. Mairi, who wore a simple apron for house-cleaning over her black skirt and blouse, couldn't stop herself from asking a question that had been weighing on her mind since Amanda had warned her about Mrs Clifford being difficult.

"Good morning Madam. I was wondering, who am I replacing in this household please? I'd like to know what happened to the girl who was here before me if you don't mind explaining."

Mairi noticed Mrs Clifford's back stiffen, but she did not lose her composure.

"No problem at all. I sacked her. I don't suffer fools gladly. Her name is not important, but she came from Wales. Let's hope Scotland will do better for England, shall we?" she added with a scornful laugh.

"Yes Madam."

The lady of the house continued. "You will have responsibility for all the housework. But I take the children for two hours every morning after breakfast. This enables Sarah to put in a good one and a half hours' sewing or more in the morning. Meanwhile, you get all your house and pantry work done before lunch. Of course, whenever there is extra work, such as preparing fruit for Christmas, jam-making or fruit bottling, I help with it."

Mrs Clifford seemed to expect a grateful smile from Mairi, but saw none.

One reason why Mairi had applied for the job, which she had found in a newspaper advertisement, was good outings, in other words perks such as some free time every day. She listened intently as Mrs Clifford started to explain the details.

"Generally Mrs Ackroyd takes the afternoon and the parlour-maid, you in other words, the evening. If you go out in the afternoon, Mrs Ackroyd must be properly dressed before she goes to answer the door, which is normally your duty. Unless we have guests, on Sundays you can both go out at the same time as you did yesterday, or in the evening, as long as you've made arrangements with Sarah. She, on the other hand, has to ask me if she wants to go out so that I may look after my little boys."

"Aye, the bairns. How old are the wee ones?"

The mention of her children seemed to soften Mrs Clifford.

"Three and five years old. Well behaved children, my dear."

They were upstairs. Mrs Clifford showed Mairi the children's bedroom, the nursery, which was down the corridor from the bedroom occupied by her and Sarah, who was thus able to be with the children quickly if something was the matter in the night. Beyond that bedroom was the master bedroom, which was where the owners of the house slept next to the family bathroom. A door shut the master bedroom and the main bathroom off from the rest of the corridor, indeed the house.

"Your duties include changing bed sheets in our bedrooms whenever necessary, and you also need to vacuum-clean the floors. Mairi, is that understood?"

"Of course Madam. I must say I've never seen a vacuum cleaner before. Where I come from we simply strew old tea-leaves on the floor."

"Tea-leaves?" Mrs Clifford was perplexed.

"Aye Madam, Tea-leaves, strained but not dry. They collect the dust and we use a broom to sweep them up. Works well."

Mrs Clifford shook her head and, with a patronising smile, said it must be hard for someone from Scotland to face modern life in England. "You've got a lot to learn, Mairi, but handling a vacuum cleaner should be easy enough even for you."

Mairi felt the insult, but said nothing.

"Any questions so far?" Mrs Clifford eyed her with interest, seemingly awaiting a reaction to her previous comment. Mairi knew better than to let her hurt show. Instead she asked:

"Who does the laundry?" That was truly hard work and Mairi dreaded the answer. She had forgotten to ask that question when she was interviewed by Mr Clifford about the job on the telephone in the post office at home.

"Oh, don't worry about the laundry. It's sent away twice a week, bed sheets, clothes, the lot. Also, don't worry about the windows. We've got a window cleaner who comes with his tall ladder."

Mrs Clifford smiled with a degree of disdain at seeing the relief in Mairi's face. "Now let's go downstairs again and I will show you the rest of the house."

Mairi had already been to the kitchen, the scullery, the main hall, the dining room with a painting of a sail boat over the fire place, and the living room, which stood out with its dark blue curtains, stately furniture and crystal chandelier. Her employer now took her through the hall into the much smaller eastern wing, where on the ground floor to the right was Mr Clifford's study and, beyond it, the morning room.

"This is where you will serve breakfast."

"Aye Madam, but how come it's called the morning room?"

"You don't know much now do you? This room is the sun pocket of the house. This is the eastern wing remember? This is where the sun rises, at least here in England. We like having some sunshine with our breakfast when the sun is out with his hat on."

Mairi bristled and felt the sting of the comment burn, but did her best to keep her composure. Mrs Clifford took her upstairs where there were two bedrooms and a bathroom for whenever guests visited and stayed the night.

"There is obviously no need for you to clean these two rooms on a daily basis. We only have guests maybe every three or four weeks, but the rooms must be spotless whenever a guest arrives. Do you understand?"

Mairi nodded without showing any emotion, but Mrs Clifford's condescending tone further angered her. What was this woman like? She couldn't have anticipated her next comment.

"By the way," Mrs Clifford continued. "Why is your name spelled in such a peculiar way? What sort of a name is it?"

"It's Scottish for Mary." Mairi spoke through clenched teeth. She wanted to give this woman a good kick.

"What's wrong with Mary?" Mrs Clifford laughed but stopped short upon seeing the flash of anger in Mairi's green eyes.

Moving to another subject, Mrs Clifford explained that St Matthias Church, just down the road in Wellswood, offered two services on Sunday mornings. "We do our best to divide what few services we have among us. Someone must always stay at home to answer the telephone and the door."

Mrs Clifford again elaborated on the outings. "Once every two weeks in the evening each girl is allowed to invite her young man for tea if she has one."

Mairi perked up.

"There are a few rules that must be kept. I must be asked at least two days before and the menfolk must be gone by 10 o'clock."

Mrs Clifford sat down in an arm chair in the living room and asked Mairi to turn on the wireless so she could listen to the news. "I suppose you've never seen one of these before. Turn the left-hand knob clockwise."

Mairi was about to make a sharp retort but managed to stay calm. Instead she said: "My father bought one of these years ago. He does enjoy listening to the news on the BBC in the evening."

Mrs Clifford appeared not to hear that last comment. As she had finished inducting Mairi she seemed to have lost interest. Or maybe she refused to acknowledge the fact that Mairi's father listened to the BBC.

"Now run along and help Mrs Ackroyd prepare breakfast."

Mairi went straight to her room rather than the kitchen. She burst into hot, angry tears and having nobody to vent her frustration on but herself, she pulled at her hair until it hurt. Her position was a dependent one, and Mrs Clifford was clearly not going to allow her to forget it.

There was a knock on the door. "Are you all right?" It was Amanda.

"I want to go home. I cannae stay here. That woman's horrid." Mairi snivelled.

Amanda opened the door and sat down with her friend, taking her hands in hers. "Problems with the mistress? I told you to stand up to her."

"She gave me some useful information, but I was totally unprepared for her humiliating comments. She kept belittling me, trying to make out that I am a complete dimwit. It's so unfair. She doesn't know me."

Amanda hugged Mairi and comforted her. "Pull yourself together and help me with the breakfast. The mistress wants you to fail. Don't give her the satisfaction."

Mairi gave away a deep sigh. "I won't fail. I will not fail my father, and I will speak my mind."

At Windsor Court, breakfast was served at eight o'clock, lunch at one o'clock, afternoon tea at four and dinner at seven in the evening, except on Sundays when supper was cold meat and a salad. There was a lot of work for a house parlourmaid who also had to make beds and clean the rooms, but Mairi was keen to prove herself before everyone in the house.

She served breakfast for the first time, not without trepidation under the critical eyes of Mrs Clifford, but Mr Clifford gave her a reassuring smile and it all went well.

Amanda and Sarah were having their breakfast in the kitchen and Mairi joined them after making sure that the family had all it needed in the morning room. The boys always had breakfast with their parents.

"How long have you worked here then?" Mairi turned to Sarah.

"Oh, just over two years, for my sins." The nurse sipped tea. "But I like it here. You just have to make sure to please Mrs Clifford."

"Aye, so I've gathered. Must be a wee bit careful around her. She seems to be difficult to please."

"By the way," Mairi said, switching to another subject. "Mrs Clifford has told me that the maid before me was from Wales, but she wouldn't say anything else. You two must have worked with her. Can you tell me about her?"

Amanda gave her a quick look and shut the kitchen door. "This is a banned subject," she whispered. "We don't discuss it. We don't discuss the inner goings-on of the family."

It was late in the evening and the Cliffords were having drinks on a couch in front of the fireplace in the living room. The rest of the house had gone to bed.

"So what do you make of her?" Mr Clifford put the question to his wife.

She smirked and had a sip of her sherry. "Well, she could have done a lot worse." Putting down her glass on the coffee table and leaning forward, she turned her gaze onto her husband. "I have seen how you look at her. You don't fool me, Raymond."

Mr Clifford put down his whisky tumbler too. "I beg your pardon. What are you insinuating, that I desire Mairi? She is only twenty, much too young for me."

His wife sat up straight as a school mistress, pursed her lips and fixed him with a look of stern reproach. "That didn't stop you from desiring Abigail, who was just twenty-two. Don't pretend that you are innocent."

She looked away. "Well, things were different in my family. My father kept a distance from the servants at home, and rightly so. They are not our equals. I will not have you demean yourself and me again. It will not do and I won't stand for it."

Mr Clifford rose and started to pace back and forth in front of the fireplace, where the shadows of the flames played an enigmatic game on the walls and ceiling. Outside an easterly wind was growing stronger, sending tree crowns swaying in the dark.

"All right Edith. We gave Abigail her notice. It's in the past for crying out loud!"

Mrs Clifford, having got the reaction she wanted, calmly settled back into her chair.

"No reason to get upset. I am only making observations and sharing them with you. I've seen Mairi blush when she looks at you. Raymond, I want you to stay clear of that girl. No small talk. Don't give her ideas above her station. I shall say no more."

Mairi was vacuum-cleaning all the main rooms except the guest rooms the following morning after serving breakfast. It was clear that no cleaning had been done for a while because dust was everywhere. She enjoyed using the electric appliance, just had to make sure to move the lead to a new socket as she made her way through the rooms or the machine would stop working. The telephone rang in the hall and she was lucky to be there or she might not have heard it amidst the din of the vacuum cleaner. She took the call, answered as instructed by the lady of the house and wrote down the message, which was from the butcher who wanted to confirm that he would deliver meat the following morning. This would please Amanda and help her plan meals.

She realised that the parquet floor in the elongated hall would be difficult to clean because there was only one light in the ceiling and the entrance hall and the back window were far apart. The same applied for the kitchen, not as a result of a lack of light, but because of the terracotta floor's unusual hexagonal pattern. Dust would get stuck in the grout between the tiles. The rest of the downstairs floors were fine though, made of parquet and illuminated by large windows.

Entering Mr Clifford's study in the east wing she was entranced by the well-stocked book shelves. Her eyes searched the spines of the books for anything she might recognise. There were many law books of course, but she noticed titles by Charles Dickens, Jane Austen and, of course, Agatha Christie, whom she knew was born in a nearby village - a local celebrity. Maybe Mr Clifford would let her borrow a book or two to save her the time going to the library? She ran her fingers across the spine of an Agatha Christie book.

Mairi was brought back to her duties by Mrs Clifford, who had been watching her from the doorway for some time. "What do you think you are doing? You are supposed to work, not stare at books. Leave my husband's study now!"

The new parlourmaid from Scotland steeled herself and walked up to Mrs Clifford, who involuntarily stepped back, not expecting to be confronted by a mere servant. They were about the same height.

"Madam, I have been brought up to say please and thank you, as everyone should, and to believe that ladies have a responsibility to behave as good employers, providing an example to their servants. I shall speak as I am spoken to, please remember that."

Mrs Clifford was clearly taken aback; she paled, glanced around the room as though seeking help, then abruptly turned and left the study.

CHAPTER THREE

Amanda and Mairi sat on their favourite bench in the back garden in late April, drinking tea after clearing away everything after lunch. Mairi had now been working at Windsor Court for a week and was settling in to the routines except she was always worried about failing to please the unsmiling Mrs Clifford.

"I thought she was going to sack me on the spot when I talked back the other day. I'm surprised I'm still here."

Amanda, who had quickly become like a big sister to Mairi, laughed. "You seem to be getting along better with her now. Good on you."

"Thanks. By the way, I do like your cooking."

Amanda shrugged. "Well, I'm a cook, it's my job."

"But I really meant what I said, your Yorkshire pudding is the best I have tasted. You're a much better cook than my mother, thank God for that."

"Why thank you, Mairi." Amanda smiled. "Speaking of your mother, why did you decide to leave home and come all the way here to work?"

Mairi squirmed. "Well, I don't think I will ever like working for Mrs Clifford, but I moved here because I wanted to seek more work experience and get around. I used to work in the post office at home, but my father suggested I go for this job, which we had seen in an advertisement in the paper."

Amanda looked her deep in the eye. She had been curious to find out more about Mairi's family situation since their walk the other day.

"Didn't you also want to get away from your mother?"

Mairi turned away from Amanda, and would say no more. Amanda had got used to her sometimes guarded manners, and let her be.

In her mind, Mairi drifted back to one of the most unpleasant confrontations with her mother.

After another day at the post office, Mairi had come home to the terraced house near the railway station. She hoped her mother, Brenda, had cooked something nice for dinner, stovies or shepherd's pie for example. But the moment she came inside her mother slapped her in the face.

"You've stolen money from my purse you filthy little thief!"

The blow stunned Mairi and she was trying to make sense of the accusation. "I haven't stolen anything. Maybe you forgot to count how much money you had!"

Her mother, a big woman with a wild tangle of wiry curls, slapped her again and started to pull her hair, like she had done so many times before. Mairi screamed in pain and kicked her mother's knee, causing the woman to moan in agony. Her father, alerted by the altercation from the living room, came rushing and separated them. A coal miner, he had considerable strength and both Mairi and her mother knew he was in charge although he'd rarely use his strength to stop them arguing.

"Not again, women! Stop this nonsense. I am sure the missing money is somewhere in the house."

After dinner, which they had in rather a tense atmosphere with Mairi suppressing angry tears at the unfairness, she sat with her father in the porch outside and they spoke quietly lest anyone would hear them.

"Father, I didn't steal anything."

He patted his daughter on the shoulder. "Of course you didn't. But your ma holds a grudge against you. We both know that."

A man on a bicycle rode past them in the street and Mairi waited until he was out of earshot. "But why? She treats my little brothers like princes, but she can't stand me. I cannae understand her problem with me."

Clyde Craig looked at his hands, so full of callouses from working in the mine, before speaking again. He was a stoic, resigned man with enough troubles on his mind, but had a soft spot for his only daughter.

"I don't want to pass judgment on you and your mother. All I know is you're both stubborn as mules."

He turned his lined face towards her. He knew his wife had always resented Mairi for her adventurous spirit and beautiful hair. "Now, I know you like working at the post office, but maybe you should consider leaving Scotland, move to England somewhere, work as a maid in a big house. Give yourself a break, learn new things."

Mairi brightened at the thought of leaving home, to see the world. At the post office she started to skim through the national papers in search of a job advertisement. She realised she didn't want to be on the lowest rung of the ladder, such as a scullerymaid. But house parlourmaid reporting to the cook seemed just right. She read advertisements where the prospective employer promised good outings. Wages were usually around 10 to 15 shillings a week, but she realised that wasn't too bad given that she'd have free food and lodging. This was how she came to apply for work at Windsor Court in a place called Torquay in Devon. She had never heard of it before, but the manager at the post office gave her good references.

Mairi was pleased to receive a letter from one Mr Clifford suggesting they talk on the telephone about her potential employment. She wrote back that she unfortunately didn't have a telephone at home, but suggested they'd speak on the telephone in the post office one evening after hours.

"Mr Clifford?" The line wasn't the best and she could just about hear him through the crackling noise.

"I hear you, Mairi. I liked your application and you seem just the right girl for the job."

Mairi trembled with excitement, not least because the man at the other end of the call had a kind and most deep and authoritative voice.

Her parents had walked her to the railway train station on a rainy morning in April and there was an emotional farewell, at least between her and her father, who wished her the best of luck in Torquay. Brenda had mixed feelings about her daughter's departure.

"You'll be back," she whispered in Mairi's ear. "The English won't have you down there. That's just the way it is."

"Mairi?" Amanda sought her attention.

"Oh, sorry. My mind was elsewhere." They were still in the garden.

"I could tell. We need to go inside now and start preparing afternoon tea."

Mairi fetched cups and plates from a cupboard in the kitchen while Amanda heated water on the cooker and prepared scones, clotted cream and jam.

Mr Clifford sat in his office at the law firm in Torquay in the afternoon looking out the window. He couldn't concentrate on work. His mind kept going back to that Saturday when he had driven his motor to the railway train station to fetch Mairi, who had looked tired after the long journey, but what had caught his attention most was her good looks. Even her shy demeanour attracted him and when she spoke he was moved by her beguiling accent. She hadn't said much on the telephone, leaving it to him to do the talking. Clever girl. They had shaken hands and he had opened the passenger door for her.

"What a lovely motor car, Mr Clifford. I do like that blue colour."

"Thanks Mairi. It's a Vauxhall. Did you have a good journey?"

"Aye Sir. So much to see in the countryside from the railway train. I brought some food with me and a book to read and I dozed off for a while." She looked out the window, observing the traffic. "I've never seen so many motor cars."

"This is nothing compared to London."

"Oh, you've been to London, Sir?"

He smiled at her enthusiastic reaction. "Once, on business."

"I changed trains in London," Mairi said. "It was a nightmare. So many people."

They fell silent, but he noticed that she glanced at him a few times and it made him feel good inside. He knew however that he had to watch himself, not flirt with her. This girl mustn't turn into another Abigail. He remembered the embarrassment when his wife had caught them in a tender embrace in the scullery of all places. He wished Edith would stop tearing into him over the scandal, which had been hushed up of course. He didn't think anyone on the council or in his law firm knew about it, but if someone dropped a hint, he would know how to shut them up. Anyway, he continued in his mind, this Scottish lass had shown realistic expectations about wages, something that earned her his respect even before he had talked to her on the phone. He knew from experience that the best servants were satisfied with the average rate of wages. They cared more for a comfortable situation with good outings and where the payments were fair and certain, rather than seeking higher remuneration than was customary. Exceptionally high wages at the outset were apt to be regarded more as a bribe than as a well-earned reward. Mairi's wishes testified to good common sense. He glanced at her profile in the car. She probably had received good advice from her father.

Breaking the silence, Mr Clifford asked Mairi if she was hungry. They had left the waterfront and he was steering uphill now. They would soon be home.

"Aye Sir. Am I too late for dinner?"

"Oh no, still plenty of time, but I'm sure Mrs Ackroyd, the cook, can fix you a sandwich and a cup of tea in the meantime." He turned to her with a reassuring smile.

His grin made her blush, which amused him.

While he respected and loved his wife he had always been drawn to younger women, who looked up to him and made him feel important. With Edith he sometimes felt as though she thought him beneath her, and maybe she was right, but she had been so pretty in her twenties and he couldn't resist asking her to marry him. The wealth in her family had attracted him too. While he was not without means, his wealth combined with hers meant he'd be guaranteed the comfort and style to which he felt entitled.

"Sir?" The junior clerk in the office asked for his attention. "Here are the court documents you ordered." Mr Clifford stopped day-dreaming and got on with his duties.

Mrs Clifford, wearing her favourite rust-red coat, had gone for a long walk in the afternoon to gather her thoughts. She couldn't get over Mairi's impertinence the other day. It was unforgivable of a domestic servant to berate her mistress like that. She sighed. Nothing, she'd read, would ever be the same after the Great War, which had helped to bring down class structures. Stopping for a moment, she remembered fondly songs such as "It's a Long Way to Tipperary" she had heard as a teenager and how she had paid three pence for a seat in the stalls to view patriotic films in Plymouth. But the modern world had changed social attitudes and expectations. There was more widespread state education and more people could read and write. They had access to the popular press, and then to the wireless and cinema. In the past ordinary people had little choice in their professions, but nowadays they were given much wider opportunities. Young women had become more reluctant than the previous generation to go into domestic service when they could easily find work in shops, factories and offices, where they didn't have to stand on ceremony. Mairi had worked in the post office in her village before deciding to go into service. Mrs Clifford wondered why – she probably had ideas above her station. Anyway, it was all about to change once she had things her way. She had to maintain day-to-day control over the servants and Mairi with her rebellious attitude didn't fit in, not to mention the way that little minx looked at her husband. Mrs Clifford smiled. She had always wanted to be in charge, she had it after her mother who had been dominated by her husband, Edith's father. To compensate, her mother had been harsh with servants, taking out her frustrations on them.

※

Back in the house Mrs Clifford went straight to her husband's study and shut the door behind her. Mr Clifford, who had just come home from work, looked up from his desk.

"Is there a problem, Edith?" He noticed the serious look on her face.

"The problem is Mairi." She gave him a meaningful stare.

He turned around in his chair to face his wife. "What has she done now?"

Mrs Clifford crossed her arms. "I caught her trying to steal a book in this room the other day. She was vacuuming the floor but I heard she had stopped so I went to see what was going on. She was pulling out a book from your shelves. I swear. I saw it."

Mr Clifford rose and walked up to the shelves. "Well, the books are all there, nothing is missing."

"Well, that's because I caught her red-handed," Mrs Clifford protested. "We should sack her now before she does any serious damage to this household. She might steal money next, or my jewellery. Who knows? I can't believe you hired her. Scots always mean trouble."

They heard steps in the hall outside the study and kept quiet until they faded away. Mr Clifford resumed the discussion. "Come on Edith. Maybe she was just curious. I've heard her talk about joining the library so she could borrow books. You keep looking for faults with Mairi, but I think she seems to be doing all right. There is no cause for getting rid of her. As you know it's hard to find good servants these days. We both know the situation on the labour market."

Mrs Clifford was about to tell her husband about the verbal clash she had had with the parlourmaid, but dignity held her back. It would be such an embarrassment to reveal that she had been rebuked by a simple servant girl. It was true that Mrs Ackroyd had once talked back a few years ago, and she had found it necessary to change her ways with the cook, not least because she was so good at her job, but this was way beyond showing respect.

"Well, as her mistress it's my job to keep an eye on her. And you stay away from small talk with that girl. I already warned you, Raymond. Don't disappoint me."

He reached out to hug her. She reluctantly gave in to his embrace. "Edith, I comprehend perfectly and I won't disappoint you."

The dinner gong rang out. Mrs Clifford followed her husband, albeit grudgingly, to the dining room where Mairi was waiting to serve them. Deep inside the lady of the house was fuming with suppressed rage. She lamented the fact that Raymond pulled the strings, being the bread winner and in charge of the household economy. He paid the wages. He had to have final say. She only wished, again, that her husband had been more like her father, not some dominant patriarch, but someone who would never have put up with this folly. Sometimes she felt she had married beneath herself. Her sister had warned her about Raymond. Yes, he was a skilled solicitor and a shrewd politician, but he was nouveau riche unlike her family, which came from Plymouth and had a long history of wealth in the fisheries industry.

She realised that she had to catch that vile servant girl out somehow one day soon, convince her feeble husband, so vulnerable to young female beauty, that Mairi indeed had to go. And, if she had to twist the knife, she could always remind him of Abigail, which she knew caused her husband pain. She had seen him flirt with her, those wandering eyes of his. Just couldn't stop himself, could he now, behaving like a cad. At least Raymond had joined the war effort as a teenage recruit in the Royal Navy, something he often boasted about. It had been a moral obligation. She recalled propaganda slogans such as: "If your young man neglects his King and Country, the time will come when he will neglect you." But although Raymond would make the most of his duties as a navy recruit, he never went to sea, never saw battle. He was all talk; that pathetic story of him fighting off a Zeppelin being a case in point.

Mrs Clifford recalled that late evening when she had gone to the scullery to look for something and as she opened the door she had found them together. Such a disgrace. She had been outraged and humiliated, but being resourceful and proud she had managed to get rid of Abigail. She would not be ousted by a mere servant - there would be no doubt about that. And now, with that Scottish girl, she would have her vengeance twice over if there were even the slightest sign of an affair.

CHAPTER FOUR

Mairi rode to the library in Lymington Road in central Torquay one afternoon in May, having borrowed a bicycle from the house to make more efficient use of her two hours off. It was a small building facing the street and she walked indoors, struck immediately by the silence and above all the dry smell of books. Rows and rows of shelves met her. She had never seen so many books in her life and was thrilled. She walked up to a shelf and put a hand on the spine of an unusually thick book. She loved reading because it provided an escape from the world around her.

She approached a desk where a young man in a blue shirt, grey tie and black trousers sat and flicked through a card index. She took the chance to look at him discreetly while he was busy, and found that she liked what she saw. He was a slim, handsome man, probably around twenty-five years old, and had thick, dark hair that she wanted to run her hands through.

"Excuse me." She coughed to draw his attention. "I would like to borrow a book, please. But how do I go about this? I have never been to a public library before. My name is Mairi Craig."

He looked up and she could read in his eyes that he warmed to her at once and had obviously caught her accent, but she worried that he had also spotted the mole in her left eyebrow.

"Hello, I'm Tristan Williams, the librarian. Let me take you through the procedure."

He asked Mairi to write down her details on a form that would make her a member so she could borrow books.

"So, what do you fancy, Miss Craig?"

"Difficult question. I just like to read, really. Maybe I should start with Agatha Christie since she was born here."

He nodded. "Good choice, how about 'The Mysterious Affair at Styles'? It was her first book and she got it published in 1920, not too long ago in other words. The main character is Monsieur Poirot, a Belgian detective who solves murder mysteries. It's a straightforward read unless you aspire to something more complicated."

Mairi eyed the book cover and touched it. "I'll start with this book thanks."

She was about to leave, heading towards the door, but turned around to say goodbye. "It was a pleasure to meet you, Mr Williams."

He winked at her. "The pleasure is all mine. Hope to see you again soon, Miss Craig."

Mairi cycled uphill in the cool evening with a big smile on her face and the book on the parcel rack. She reminded herself that she needed a new coat.

Amanda and Mairi again sat on the bench in the garden during a break, reading books and drinking lemonade they'd brought with them. They watched the gardeners, Steve and Jim, hard at work now that the lawns and the flowers, as well as the weeds, were coming into full bloom. Steve, a young broad-shouldered blond man, would mow the lawns, do the edging and cut the hedges while Jim, who was older, shorter and frailer, was the senior gardener in charge of the orchard, including the greenhouse. The Cliffords prided themselves in being more or less self-sufficient with fruits, berries and vegetables grown in their gardens, which covered about two acres.

"Where do Steve and Jim live?" Mairi looked at the men with curiosity. She had started going for walks in the gardens in her spare time when she wasn't off to the town centre on her breaks, and she had seen the gardeners at work.

"Oh, they live nearby and cycle to work whenever the garden needs tending, which is practically every day now that spring is here. They also take delivery of coal to the house as you've seen."

Mairi turned to Amanda. "Is this the life you want for yourself? Working for the Cliffords for ever, like Sarah seems prepared to do?"

"Oh no! I want to get married, have children. I do have a boyfriend. I might invite him for tea one evening so you get to see him."

"Aye, what's his name? Is he from here?" Mairi got curious but also felt a sting of envy in her heart.

"His name is Steve, like one of them gardeners and blond as well. He's from Paignton like me. He works as a cook in a restaurant there, so we're both interested in food. We're a good match I hope."

Mairi's thoughts went to Tristan Williams, but her mind was also on Mr Clifford, with his kind smiles and jovial nature. "Does it happen that men who own a house marry a servant girl?"

Amanda looked up from her book. "Oh yes! Let me tell you a story, a legendary one. There once was a land owner in Sussex whose name was Sir Harry. He used to be a famous rake, a friend of the Prince Regent and a lover of Lady Emma Hamilton."

"When was this then?" Mairi was keen to hear all the details.

"Oh, a hundred years ago."

Amanda went on to explain that Sir Harry, in his later years, overheard a girl singing on his estate at Uppark. His housekeeper, when asked about the singer, told him it was one of the dairy maid's helpers. When the old dairy maid retired she was replaced by Mary Ann Bullock, the object of his desire.

"Sir Harry asked the girl to marry him, although she was fifty years younger. It must have shocked her to get such a proposition, but he got her interested. 'Don't answer me now, but if you will have me, cut a slice out of the leg of mutton that is coming up for my dinner tonight.'"

The mutton arrived with a slice cut out, much to the irritation of the cook, but to the delight of Sir Harry. Once she had accepted, Mary Ann was sent off to Paris where she learnt to read, write and embroider. They married at Uppark in September 1825. Sir Harry was said to have told his gamekeeper: "I've made a fool of myself."

"Aye, like my father says. There is no fool like an old fool. But was it a happy marriage?" Mairi was excited.

"I've heard it was. Mary Ann cared for him until his death about twenty years later at the age of ninety-something, and he left her all his possessions. Fancy!"

"Goodness." Mairi shook her head in disbelief. "Like a fairy tale."

Amanda, realising she had a keen listener, said she knew of another example. "I can't remember all the details, but there was a landowner in Nottinghamshire. He fell in love with the nursery housemaid, a young woman nicknamed Polly if I remember. She had a great dress sense apparently and somehow knew how to run a household. People who came for a visit didn't know her background. They saw her as the lady of the manor. She gave her husband seven sons, but I'm afraid six of them died in the Great War."

"Six of them died?" Mairi fell silent and read her book for a while. But she couldn't leave the subject of wealthy men proposing to young women.

"Hang on a minute! Let me guess. Mr Clifford had an affair with that Welsh girl, right?"

"You mean Abigail?"

"Oh, was that her name?"

"Mairi, you are being naughty. You made me say it. You must keep this secret to yourself."

"Call me Madame Poirot."

"Madame what?"

Mairi grinned in triumph. "I've borrowed this book by the crime writer Agatha Christie at the library. Surely you must know of her. She writes about a detective called Monsieur Poirot. Now I feel like a detective too. By the way, the librarian is a nice young man with dark thick hair."

Amanda raised an eyebrow, intrigued by the mention of the young librarian. But she rose from the bench and stood over Mairi, wagging a finger at her.

"I will tell you what happened, but you must never spread a word about it or we can kiss goodbye to our work in this house. Promise me that, Mairi!"

"Aye Amanda. Please tell me."

The cook gave away a sigh. "All right. Here's what happened. Mrs Clifford apparently had her suspicions that her husband had an affair with Abigail from Wales. She looked a bit like you I guess, which could mean them alarm bells are ringing in the head of Mrs

Clifford again. Not another pretty house parlourmaid falling for her husband. Not your fault."

Mairi, feeling a blush of pride at this compliment on her looks, swept back a lock with her hand.

Amanda sat down again and, after due reflection, continued. "Point is Mrs Clifford caught them in a romantic situation somewhere in the house." She waited to gauge Mairi's reaction, who blushed and giggled with shock and delight at such a thing.

"Anyway, to cut a long story short as they say, Abigail was sacked but given compensation, really a bribe of something like £20 to shut up. She told me just before she left. Fancy £20!"

The only trouble was, Abigail received no reference from the Cliffords, which meant she would have difficulties finding another job, having worked here for a full year with no record to show for it.

"She certainly needed the money, but she wouldn't last long without an income," Amanda concluded.

Mairi put a hand to her mouth. "I hear you. Must keep a distance from Mr Clifford so his wife doesn't start thinking that we're having an affair. Being fired without a reference would be the worst thing that could happen to me. My parents would be so disappointed."

Amanda returned to reading her book, but Mairi sat in deep thought for a long while.

Amanda had gone to bed with a book she was half-way through, but it bored her and her mind drifted to Mairi, a lively girl although she had her quiet moments, no doubt because of the conflict she had hinted at with her mother back home. The new colleague was otherwise dependable and good to work with, and Amanda was glad to have someone closer to her age in the house again after Abigail had left.

The cook recalled the days when tension filled the house over Mrs Clifford's suspicions that her husband was having an affair with Abigail, and then the rows that followed the moment she had caught them together. Amanda counted the days on her fingers, it had only been four weeks ago. Abigail had been out of the house in a hurry. Those had been trying days when the Cliffords had to hire an inexperienced young woman in the neighbourhood as a temporary help who had to shoulder some of the tasks of a house parlourmaid, sharing them with Sarah. Mrs Clifford had continued to make life a misery for her husband, but she started to calm down soon after Abigail had been given her marching orders. As part of the deal she had made with the Cliffords, she had gone back to Wales because Mrs Clifford didn't want to run into her in Torquay.

Amanda enjoyed working at Windsor Court because Mr Clifford was a good boss. The pay wasn't much to write home about but job security and comfortable terms such as time off every day meant more to her. But one day soon she would want to leave the Cliffords, marry Steve and move in with him in Paignton. She was getting older and she wanted children. Most of her friends were already mothers. All in due time. Amanda put away the book and switched off the bedside lamp.

One Sunday morning after breakfast Mairi was wandering from room to room in the house, which was empty except for herself and Amanda. The Cliffords had gone to the first church service at eight o'clock with their little boys and Sarah and when they came back home to Windsor Court it was going to be time for Amanda and Mairi to attend the second service at half past ten.

Mairi walked from the kitchen to the big hall and up the main stairway past old sepia brown family photos on the left wall. She stopped at what must, by the look of them, be Mrs Clifford's parents around the turn of the century. They were dressed up and stared solemnly at the camera. Amanda had told her both were deceased. She continued up the stairs to the landing where she strode down to the master bedroom. She had yet to make the bed for the Cliffords. A picture from their wedding some years ago adorned a chest of drawers. The mistress looked happy. Mairi again worried about her recent spat with Mrs Clifford and that the lady might find an excuse to have her sacked. Madam had not been openly rude to Mairi since she had stood up to her but her intuition said that the woman could well be biding her time; after all, she was more likely to bear a grudge than develop a respect for her. Mairi pulled out a piece of cloth from her apron to wipe the dust from the mantel piece over the fire place. It seemed that the coal fires left dust everywhere but as of this weekend Mr Clifford had decided there would be no more fires in the house until autumn.

It was a ten-minute walk down Warberry Hill to St Matthias Church, a grey 19th century stone building in Wellswood.

"Do you go to church in Lanarkshire?" Amanda turned to Mairi as they entered the church.

"Of course we do, but I must say this church is much bigger than the one at home." Mairi craned her neck to marvel at the off-white arches as well as the dark-wood panelling in the ceiling.

They sat down near the front on the left-hand side and Mairi noticed that the vicar, a short man in his sixties with a shock of white hair, had seen her. He gave her a gentle nod in acknowledgement, which she shyly returned. She assumed that he would always recognise a new church-goer and the church was only a quarter-full so spotting her reddish blonde hair was easy for him. The organ, situated to the right of the altar, came to life with a rousing chord and everyone rose to sing a hymn - O worship the King all glorious above.

Mairi admired the limestone pillars and the colourful stained glass windows on the left-hand side of the altar with their depictions of Moses with the Ten Commandments and the coat of arms of Queen Victoria. She didn't recognise any of the other figures or motifs on the windows. She whispered a prayer asking God for forgiveness for her shortcomings and prayed that the Lord make Mrs Clifford treat her with kindness. The mistress was a regular church-goer and something of the message of love from Christ must surely rub off on her. At least that was the wish of an innocent twenty-year-old parlourmaid from Scotland.

Things were busy for Amanda and Mairi at lunch time because Mr Clifford had invited two close Tory confidants from the council who had arrived with their wives. Amanda had to cook Sunday roast for four more people than normal and the dining table was full. Everyone had a jolly good time and as the three couples finished their meals Mairi entered to clear away the plates ahead of pudding. Mairi hadn't quite got the hang of it yet to pile several plates up her arm and one, a beautiful white-and-blue plate, slipped through her hand and went crashing to the floor.

"Mairi! Would you be more careful! You just broke a piece of fine china, the cost of which will come straight out of your wages." Mrs Clifford gave Mairi a withering look that to her seemed out of proportion to what had clearly been an accident. But she was determined to make the mistress warm to her.

"Awfully sorry, Madam." Mairi picked up the pieces and retreated to the kitchen where Amanda gave her a comforting smile.

Pausing in the kitchen, she cursed herself for having dropped that plate, wondering how much it would cost to replace. But on the whole she thought she'd done all right serving lunch for so many people. She had been nervous early on working at the post office at home, too, but had then gone from strength to strength and the postmaster had been pleased with her work. She told herself she'd be fine. Stop believing in yourself and no one else will.

Sarah, having fed the boys, helped Mairi wait on tables as the men stayed in the dining room after luncheon for political discussions over coffee, cognac and cigars while the women retreated to the living room for coffee and sherry.

"Anything new?" This was one of Mr Clifford's favourite opening gambits in a discussion. He had found that it always got people talking. Sitting back comfortably with his fingertips together, he eyed his guests.

"Well, what do we make of Mosley?" Mr Parker, a dandy with a red silk vest and a pin-stripe dark suit, was arranging his moustache with exquisite care. "Should we talk to him or not?"

Oswald Mosley was looking into making Plymouth headquarters in the West Country for his fledgling British Union of Fascists. The port city was a mere thirty-five miles southwest of Torquay.

"Well, what with national unemployment at more than twenty-two percent, Mosley might attract voters with his protectionist, nationalist policies," suggested Mr Taylor, a fair-haired councillor who at fifty was the oldest of the three gentlemen. He adjusted his gold-rimmed pince-nez.

Mr Clifford puffed on his cigar. "Quite so, quite so, old boy, but I somehow dislike those black shirts that Mr Mosley employs at his street rallies. They remind me of Hitler's rowdy brown shirts and there is something distinctively primitive and anti-intellectual about them. I wouldn't want to be surrounded by hooligans."

Mairi, pouring more coffee and cognac, smiled at Mr Clifford. She liked hearing the gentlemen talk about politics.

"Also," he continued, his voice pregnant with significance. "We're starting to come out of the depression and unemployment will start to drop. Mark my words."

Mairi disappeared into the kitchen.

"Pretty girl that new maid," Mr Parker observed, dabbing at his lips with his napkin. "I adore her Scottish accent. She would make the most trivial subject sound erotic."

Mr Clifford smiled. "Yes, she is rather charming, and a good egg too. By the way, will you join me on the boat on Saturday morning? It's good weather for sailing now."

"Most kind of you. We're both up for it, aren't we gentlemen?" Mr Taylor eyed Mr Parker, who nodded in agreement.

The luncheon was over and the Taylors and Parkers prepared to leave. They all trooped out through the hall. The throb of the motor came through the open window and the guests all climbed into their black chauffeur-driven saloon, its tyres crunching on the gravel driveway as the driver engaged first gear and released the clutch.

It was late in the afternoon and Mairi realised that she had forgotten to vacuum the floor in Mr Clifford's study, or maybe, she confessed to herself, she was just reluctant to do it for fear of being confronted by Madam there again. She took out the vacuum cleaner from the storage space underneath the stairs and crossed the hall. She would make sure not to touch a single book again and, anyway, Mrs Clifford had gone for a walk in the afternoon sun with her little boys. She came across as a good mother who doted on her sons, something which had struck Mairi as a paradox given her otherwise authoritative style and need to have the upper hand at all times. Mairi entered the study only to find Mr Clifford at his desk reading documents. He looked up with a broad grin that made her feel uneasy.

"Och. Sorry Sir. I can come back later. Didn't mean to disturb you." She turned around to leave, but he gestured for her to stay.

"Carry on by all means, Mairi. It won't take you a minute to do the floor in my little study. I can certainly stand the noise and I'm pleased to see you going about your duties even on a Sunday afternoon."

"Aye Sir. I'll be out of here before you know it." She turned on the vacuum cleaner.

Mairi felt his eyes were on her movements and this unwelcome interest made her truly uncomfortable. He had never before shown this almost creepy side of him, but she knew he had had one glass of hock and two glasses of cognac during the luncheon. Mindful of what had happened to Abigail, she avoided eye contact for fear of encouraging him.

Mairi switched off the vacuum cleaner and wiped dust off the book shelves and the window sill - those eyes of his still on her. Thank God Mrs Clifford had gone for a walk or she would have hit the ceiling seeing the house parlourmaid alone with her husband, regardless of how innocent the circumstances were. By chance, Mairi looked through the window and to her horror noticed that Madam was back in the driveway with the boys.

"Well, this room is finished. Must leave now, Sir." She gave him a quick glance before hurrying back to the hall with the vacuum cleaner, putting it back under the stairs as she heard the key in the door.

Mairi sprinted back to the rear hall, past the kitchen and up the servants' narrow stairway to the landing, closing the door to the bedroom behind her. From downstairs came the voices of Mrs Clifford and her sons going about their business. She took a deep breath; the last thing she wanted was to be seen by that woman in the hall within a few steps of Mr Clifford in his study. She found a towel in the cupboard and wiped the sweat from her face. She sat down on the bed, having calmed down and breathing normally again. She had seen disappointment in Mr Clifford's eyes as she left his study.

CHAPTER FIVE

"Have you ever tasted a Mars bar?" Amanda and Mairi were about to buy tickets and sweets at the pictures in the evening as a reward to themselves after all the hard work during the Sunday luncheon.

"What is it?" Mairi gave the black-and-red wrapping a suspicious look.

"Oh, it's a new sweet, chocolate with nougat and caramel. I'll treat you to one. Now let's go inside and watch the film."

They sat down halfway back in the cinema and Mairi was amazed at how big the silk screen was. They were going to see "All Quiet on the Western Front", an American film based on a book by the German writer Erich Maria Remarque about the Great War. It was in black and white and they really had wanted to see something romantic in technicolour, which was a new invention, but this war film was the only one available on this Sunday night.

The Pathé newsreel opened with King George V appearing at some recent official function in London. Mairi turned to Amanda and whispered: "What's this? I thought we were going to see a film about the war?"

"Shhh. This is the newsreel. Always comes up before the big picture."

The next news item was about the Reichstag fire in Berlin on February 27. Dark views were shown of the interior of the badly damaged parliamentary building. Firemen looked around and played water hoses on the remains. Exterior shots showed fire damage to the glass roof.

The film itself left Mairi disturbed. The meaningless killing, young men who could have had long lives ahead of them starting families, looking after their parents, suddenly shooting each other to pieces in a relentless trench war where hundreds of soldiers died on both sides for the mere advance of maybe 200 yards, soon to be lost again. The darkness, the rain, the barbed wire, the artillery, screams in agony, men turned into cannon fodder by their military superiors based far away, not to mention the politicians in the respective capitals. The horrors of modern warfare. She had known very little about the grim details of the Great War, and the Germans had started it! Shaken, she abruptly left the cinema hall halfway through the film.

Amanda caught up with Mairi outside later. "Look, I know this wasn't a love story, but we paid good money to see this film - it's a shame you missed the end. It was dramatic, yes, but I guess one can learn from watching it."

Mairi, who had been waiting outside deep in thought, had tears in her eyes. "What can we learn from this slaughter? That it should never happen again? Aye, but I don't need to spend a whole damn evening to have that rubbed in."

Because they had half an hour before they had to go back home and it was still early evening, they went to a tea house for tea, scones, clotted cream and strawberry jam. Seated by a window overlooking the bustling Union Street, they gave their orders to a young waitress.

"So great to be served for once," Mairi observed.

"Mairi, you've been here more than three weeks now. Do you like Torquay?"

The parlourmaid's face lit up. "Och, I do like it very much. There is a pub in my village, but not a tea house like this. Maybe five hundred people live in my village but here they must number several thousand. Look out the window at all these people in the street. And I like the library and the cinema, just depends on what's showing. But I could eat a Mars bar every day."

Amanda smiled. "I suppose this is a lively place for you but I grew up around here and Torquay can be really dull, especially in winter when the house-owners from London are gone. A lot of them keep a holiday home here you know. Started in Victorian times."

Mairi was amazed. "You mean people who live in London can afford to have another home down here?"

"Some, yes. But in winter this tea house is shut."

Mairi looked out the window with dreamy eyes. "There must be an opportunity for women like you and me, something better, where we get more respect. I just don't see it happening any time soon, and I remain worried about my job here."

Coming home, they ran into Mr Clifford in the hall and he was curious to know what film they had watched.

"All Quiet on the Western Front," Amanda informed him. "Except Mairi stormed out halfway through the film."

"You stormed out?" he looked at the house parlourmaid while he lit his pipe, giving her a strange, knowing smile that Amanda couldn't avoid noticing.

"Aye Sir. I couldn't bear watching that slaughter of men. But we saw newsreels before the film and I thought the fire in the Reichstag a weird thing to watch. Why would anyone want to burn down a parliament building?"

"Good question Mairi." Mr Clifford gave her an appreciative look. "Still showing it are they? I guess they do because Hitler is very much in the news."

Mairi nodded, but avoided his gaze: "I read that Mr Hitler came to power in Germany following elections in January. He has since taken over the country completely."

Mr Clifford was astounded. "You seem to read a lot, Mairi."

"Aye Sir, gives me comfort."

"Comfort against what?"

"This cruel world, Sir. I'm talking about literature, not newspapers, but I read them too. I'm proud that I can read and write. Not everyone is able to."

Mr Clifford wanted to enquire further, but his wife entered the room and their discussion froze on the spot.

"So you girls came home in one piece after the cinema. Shouldn't you go to bed?"

"Yes Madam," said Amanda.

Mairi said nothing, her mind still being on the war film.

"We were just discussing Hitler," Mr Clifford said. "They saw a newsreel about the Reichstag fire in Berlin."

"Oh Hitler, at least he creates work," Mrs Clifford commented. "People should work more." she added, with a meaningful glance at Mairi, who couldn't be bothered to rise to the bait.

"But the question is whether or not a strong Germany is in our favour," Mr Clifford suggested. "After all, we fought the huns in the war and we wouldn't want them to rearm. We don't want another war. I was in the Royal Navy in the war."

The young women looked at him with interest. "Did you see battle, Sir?" Amanda asked.

"I did shore duty. Joined the Navy in 1917 as a teenager. Served in Plymouth, at Devonport Naval Base to be exact. I once came under attack from a Zeppelin airship. It was quite an experience, being bombed. I opened fire with my rifle of course, but the thing flew away. I am happy to be alive."

"Sir, that must have been terribly exciting," Amanda said.

Mr Clifford smiled at her, but Mrs Clifford cringed, although nobody noticed it. Mairi looked less impressed, too.

"The Germans will rearm and attack us again if they want to," she said with sudden conviction. "We cannae stop them. They're bad people."

Everyone looked at her with astonishment. Mairi herself was taken by surprise at her statement.

Mrs Clifford had had quite enough. "Now off to bed girls. You need your sleep."

"There is more to that girl than meets the eye," commented Mr Clifford as he put out the light in the master bedroom.

Mrs Clifford gave him a dark look. "I told you not to engage in small talk with her."

"But she was with Mrs Ackroyd and we had a civilised discussion."

"Civilised? She didn't even recognise my presence in the room!" Mrs Clifford was fuming again. She knew however that she would get her revenge somehow. No servant girl would ever humiliate her again, that Scottish bitch could count on that.

✦

"Mr Clifford likes you. I've seen how he looks at you. Are you going to make a move?" Amanda teased Mairi over breakfast.

Mairi gave the cook an angry look. "I'm in enough trouble with Mrs Clifford as it is, thanks to you."

Amanda threw her hands into the air. "Drat, I was only giving you sound advice. If you overdid it when you talked back, that's your problem."

Mairi wanted to give Amanda a good kick, but wouldn't dream of doing it to her friend and immediate boss of course. It was just something that she felt like doing when she was frustrated, kicking someone hard, better than pulling her own hair. It wasn't her fault if Mr Clifford looked at her in the wrong sort of way. She explained to Amanda what had happened in his study in the afternoon after the Sunday luncheon.

"Gosh. I never knew that Mr Clifford could be like that, what's the word, predatory? He always struck me as a true gentleman, as I told you when we went on that walk on your first Sunday morning here. Puts Abigail in a different light, doesn't it? He really did actively seduce her then. It wasn't as if they were drawn to each other over a period of time, which I always thought. But you did well not to encourage him and what a scene Mrs Clifford would have created had you not been so quick." Amanda laughed but, realising that Mairi couldn't see the funny side, became serious again.

"Anyway." Mairi returned to the previous subject. "It's true that Mrs Clifford treats me better now since my complaint, but I can see her evil eyes on me sometimes when she doesn't think I am aware. She is trying to get me into trouble. That's just the way she is."

Sarah joined them in the kitchen. "Oh stop it. We all work for Mrs Clifford. Don't make a fuss. We are in the same boat, all three of us."

Amanda gave Sarah a sympathetic look. "I know. We live in a grim world, what with the depression. So much unemployment. We should all count our blessings that we've got work."

Sarah and Mairi made noises of agreement.

Mairi borrowed a bicycle from the house again on a Tuesday to ride down to the library and return the book, hoping to see Tristan. Thinking about the Great War, she wondered again what had been so great about it. Couldn't God have stopped it? As for herself, in her own little world, she felt as if she wasn't being given a proper chance to find happiness. Her mind drifted back to one morning years ago when she stood in front of the mirror in the hall at home and studied her face from different angles. She wanted to buy lipstick, but her mother had dismissed her wish as vanity. As she stood there, she saw her mother walking up from behind.

"Stop looking yourself in the mirror, girl! Try to be useful in the household for a change. The floor in the living room needs cleaning. Get on with it."

"Aye ma, but I was only having a look at myself. No harm in that."

Her mother shrugged. "You think you're pretty. Well, I don't think so. You are just a vain, lazy lass who needs a beating from time to time. Now go and do something useful with yourself!"

Mairi shut her eyes at the memory of that moment when her mother had caned her for talking back; the humiliation, the pain, the tears. Not even at school had she endured corporal punishment, but home was a different matter. And now her cruel mother had been replaced by another unforgiving female authority out to get her. But Mairi was grown up now; she must try and learn to defend herself.

Mairi stopped thinking about the past and concentrated on cycling through a street crossing. She leaned the bicycle against a post and went up to the library entrance, only to find out that it was shut on Tuesday afternoons. She grabbed the bicycle and was about to ride up the hill again when she spotted Tristan, wearing a grey flat cap and matching clothes walking with a dark blonde girl in a smart red dress down the street. Mairi hid behind a tree until they had gone round the corner. She winced and rode uphill with tears in her eyes. What a fool she'd been for allowing herself to think she'd have a chance at happiness with Tristan. Maybe her mother had been right, she was just a vain, stupid girl. She had no right to be happy.

"Did you see that handsome librarian again?" Amanda turned around as Mairi came into the kitchen.

"What librarian? Did I ever mention a librarian?" Mairi began to take out cups and plates for afternoon tea from a cupboard with great determination.

Amanda gave her a lingering look, but knew better than to push Mairi. She could be a sensitive thing sometimes.

Everything ambled on without any hitches for the rest of the day, and in the evening Amanda and Mairi chatted over a cup of tea in the kitchen.

"You know I mentioned Steve, my boyfriend. He is coming for tea next Tuesday evening. I've got permission from Mrs Clifford. You'll get a chance to see him."

"That would be nice." Mairi spoke without conviction.

Mairi was mopping the floor in the living room the following morning when Mrs Clifford called on her from the hall. With a sinking feeling in her chest she joined the mistress.

"Is there something wrong Madam?"

Mrs Clifford gave her that withering look she had got used to. Here we go again, she thought.

"The floor isn't clean. There is dust in the corners here and there everywhere. Clean it!"

Mairi looked around but couldn't see any dust. "But Madam, I just mopped it and it is a bit dark here in the hall. You know that."

"So you are making excuses?" Mrs Clifford was livid. "Finish the living room and then come back here and start all over in the hall until I am satisfied with your work. I don't care how long it takes. Understood?"

"Aye Madam." Mairi gave away a deep sigh.

"Oh, and Mairi, you'd better clean the kitchen floor again and again. There is still dirt in the grout between the tiles. Do you need tea-leaves to do a proper job? We could gather some after tea time today. We could all join in." Mrs Clifford laughed.

"It will be done, Madam." Mairi spoke through gritted teeth. She tried her best not to let her tormentor see the hurt in her eyes. "But you could be more polite, like saying please, if you remember what we talked about."

Madam left the hall in a huff.

After lunch Mairi rode back to the library, knowing she must return the book or be fined. Walking inside, she found Tristan there talking to an elderly woman and queued up behind her. Seeing him again was hurtful and she wanted to run away, but instead waited for her turn. Tristan had noticed she was there of course and she realised he was trying to finish his conversation with the woman as quickly as possible.

"Hi Miss Craig, so nice to see you again. How was the book?"

"Not very good afraid. I came to return it. Here it is. I won't be borrowing books again."

His eyes widened in disbelief. "Is something the matter?"

Mairi turned around and hastened towards the exit, but Tristan ran after her and blocked the door. "I'm overjoyed to see you again. What's happening here?"

She became blushed, suddenly uncertain. "I came to return the book yesterday afternoon and saw you walking away with a woman in red."

"Oh, you mean Jane. That's my sister."

"Your sister?"

"Yes, I had just shut the library and she came to fetch me because we were going to buy a birthday present for our mother. She will be sixty tomorrow."

Relief flooded through Mairi and hope filled her heart once more. Suddenly the door opened and a middle-aged man with a big beard walked inside with a bag full of books. Tristan whispered: "Mairi, please take a seat here by the wall and let me help this customer. He is a regular. Then we'll talk again, OK?"

Mairi was still a bit sceptical and happy to have a respite, a moment to herself. She wanted to believe him, he did look honest. It struck her that if the woman in red was indeed his sister she would find out sooner or later if she started going out with him.

Tristan came over and sat down next to her. "I swear Jane is my sister. I don't have a girlfriend. Do you have a boyfriend, Miss Craig?"

Mairi blushed. "Of course not. I must make my apologies for acting silly."

Tristan looked rather pleased to have found out she was not attached, and smiled in return.

She took a deep breath. "By the way, please call me Mairi. And would you like to come for tea at Windsor Court one evening? We're allowed to invite menfolk once in a while. I could show you the whole house, the rooms where I work. It's a big house and you'd be impressed by all the duties I have. Amanda the cook is having her boyfriend over in a few days. If you agree I could ask the mistress for a convenient hour, usually on Tuesday evenings."

Tristan took her hand in his and the contact sent a surge of pleasure through her body that left her momentarily breathless.

"Of course. I'd be delighted." He smiled.

Mairi borrowed another book by Agatha Christie and found herself flying back up the hill beaming all over and crying tears of joy this time in between.

CHAPTER SIX

One morning after breakfast Mrs Clifford ran into Mrs Ackroyd in the hall and asked her to come to her husband's study. Amanda followed her with curiosity and they sat down in the room, Mrs Clifford in her husband's chair and the cook in another.

"I shall go straight to the point, Mrs Ackroyd." The mistress took a deep breath and started what to her listener sounded like a well-rehearsed speech. "It's about Mairi, obviously. I'm not happy with her service. She doesn't keep the floors as clean as they should be. She is untidy and sloppy in general and she doesn't make the beds properly. In addition, she has on occasion been rude to me and I have seen how she casts longing eyes on my dear husband."

She paused to gauge the reaction from her cook. "Now, I seem to have difficulties persuading my husband to take action as a result of my complaints …"

"Take action?" Amanda interrupted her, not understanding what Mrs Clifford was getting at.

"Dismissal. I am talking about sending Mairi on her way back to Scotland on the railway train, third-class of course."

Amanda put a hand to her mouth. "With all respect Mrs Clifford but that sounds harsh to me."

"Well, sometimes we have to take resolute steps to correct a problem. You know how quickly we dealt with Abigail. But I have asked you here because I want to know your opinion on the house parlourmaid. She works directly under you. Can you trust her? Do you keep having to remind her of her duties in the kitchen? That sort of thing. If you have even the slightest complaint about her I could add it to my list and present it to Mr Clifford. He can just about bat away my grievances, but if you share some of my views he'd have to recognise we have a serious problem with the new parlourmaid."

Amanda was stunned, speechless at first, but then she spoke with conviction. "Mrs Clifford. I'm sorry, but I can't say that I have got any problems with Mairi. Like any other maid new to the job she had a lot to learn and made mistakes in the first few days, but now she has settled in and I enjoy working with her."

Mrs Clifford looked more dissatisfied than she normally did. "Thank you Mrs Ackroyd. That will be all. And this discussion stays between you and me, understood?"

"Of course Mrs Clifford. Now if I am excused I need to get back to the kitchen."

"Off you go then."

Amanda did an inventory of the larder to see what was running out. They were short of potatoes, celeriac and carrots, oh, and onions too, so those vegetables needed be added to the purchase list for the greengrocer in Wellswood. Later, in the summer, she would be able to harvest many vegetables from the garden, but for now she had to rely on the greengrocer. She tried to concentrate but in her mind she kept returning to the shocking conversation she had just had with Mrs Clifford. That woman was dangerous and to think that she was trying to spin a yarn that Mairi was useless. It was beyond the pale. Well, the mistress would not get any support from the kitchen. Imagine Mairi, often bubbly but oversensitive at times, kicked out and sent home without references. It would break the poor girl's heart. Amanda decided she must certainly keep that conversation with Mrs Clifford to herself because she knew that Mairi would be terribly upset and worried if she realised what was going on in the mind of that wicked woman. Amanda recalled the afternoon when she had put her foot down after Mrs Clifford had complained about her cooking, saying it wasn't savoury enough, and suggesting ways of improvement. The mistress had written down a recipe of her own for steak and kidney pie that she insisted Amanda should use. She had looked at it with a wry smile because some of the ingredients had been wrong or the measurements not right. Amanda had explained all this to Mrs Clifford, who realised that the cook knew better than her and she had backed off, but it had been a typical example of her attempts to control everything and find faults in other people. Since then Amanda had never had any complaints from the mistress of the house.

Mairi couldn't stop tapping her feet in time to the beat and it surprised her in a good way. She was at the cinema on a Sunday night with Tristan. They were watching an American technicolour film titled "King of Jazz" and which featured crooner Bing Crosby. The film didn't have much of a story but the music blew her away. She had never heard jazz before. She was amazed. She even spotted negro musicians in the band. During a slow love song, romance entered her young life as Tristan took her hand in his and nuzzled her ear. The contact sent shivers down her spine and she cuddled up to him in the seats.

As they left the cinema Mairi was too shy to mention their brief touch and Tristan seemed content to leave it as a sweet memory. They had all the time in the world to get to know each other, and share more moments of bliss, or so it seemed.

"You liked the film then, Mairi?" He took a deep breath of fresh evening air.

"Och, I loved it. Didn't you notice how I couldn't keep my feet still during those fast swing tunes? This was something new to me and I wouldn't mind seeing another film with that Bing Crosby. He has a wonderful voice."

Tristan nodded. "Yes indeed, but there are critics who oppose the influx of American films. They condemn what they call the 'Americanisation' of British culture, but I wouldn't be too worried about that. I like America. They helped us in the war you know."

The mentioning of the war didn't go down well with Mairi who recalled that horrible film she had been to see with Amanda, but she did her best not to let it show. They came to a street corner where their ways parted. Tristan was going to catch the bus to his home in Paignton while Mairi was headed up the road to Windsor Court. They looked at each other in some kind of waiting game. Finally, Tristan took her in his arms and hugged her.

"Good night my Scottish princess," he whispered in her ear and kissed her cheek.

"Good night my prince," she whispered back with a smile.

As she walked away she stopped for a final look at him and he turned around as well. They waved at each other in mutual warmth and delight. Such a sweet summer evening it was, one that Mairi would never forget in her short life.

It was a Tuesday evening and menfolk were allowed in for tea with their loved one at Windsor Court.

"Well, hello Mr Smith, good to see you again." Mrs Clifford patted Steve, Amanda's boyfriend, on the shoulder. "I like your brown jacket and those beige trousers, you dress well."

Mairi had opened the tradesmen's entrance, the back door down the hall from the kitchen, as he rang the bell. She liked him at once, his blond hair, his gait, his casual manners. He looked like a young man who stood his ground, but she figured he was no better than Tristan. They were just different.

Amanda introduced them. "Steve dear, this is Mairi, our new parlourmaid from Scotland."

"Really, all the way from Scotland?" Steve took in Mairi's appearance. "I've never met anyone from Scotland before. How do you do?"

They shook hands and all three of them sat down at the kitchen table. Mrs Clifford left the room.

"So, are you getting married?" Mairi couldn't help popping the question.

"Oh, let's not get ahead of ourselves." Steve grinned.

"But it's certainly something that's on our mind," Amanda filled in with a degree of resolve that wasn't lost on Mairi.

Mairi, always being practical and direct to a fault, asked who would do the cooking, both of them being professional cooks?

Amanda and Steve glanced at each other and seemed to find the situation hilarious. He gave Amanda a look that appeared to ask for permission to speak for both of them. Mairi was thrilled.

"All right. If or when we get married I suppose Amanda will do the cooking. I will come home after cooking all day and I guess

Amanda will be looking after the household and," he glanced at her again, "one day the children if we are blessed."

Mairi felt a wonderful warmth inside.

After Steve had gone and it was bedtime, Mairi stole away to the living room where she knew Mrs Clifford was sitting reading a book – her husband was in his study – and she had an urgent question on her mind.

"Madam, before we all go to bed, may I ask if I could have a young man over for tea one evening soon?"

Mrs Clifford frowned. "How long have you known him?"

"Oh, about two weeks. He is the librarian. His name is Tristan Williams. We went to the cinema together the other night."

"You shouldn't rush into these things, you know." Mrs Clifford remained reluctant.

Mairi couldn't believe what the woman was on about: "But to get to know him I need to see him and I'm sure he would love to meet you."

"Let me think about it."

Mairi felt her heart sink. She knew Mrs Clifford was testing her on purpose. Why would she refuse her this chance at happiness? She felt her anger bubble up.

"But Madam, I thought this was an unquestionable outing for us servants."

"You have to earn it. Ask again in a month or two."

Mairi was in disbelief. The cow was trying to use her weakness, her wish for love, to her own advantage. The bubble of hope she'd been floating on since seeing Tristan again had burst, leaving her feeling deflated and frustrated with her lack of power to do anything about the situation. The servant girl went to her bedroom and started pulling at her hair in frustration until it hurt just as Sarah entered.

"What on earth are you doing? Stop it."

Mairi cried at Sarah's shoulder. "You and Amanda are the only women who seem to understand me."

"There now, tell me what the matter is."

Mairi poured her heart out, and Sarah listened to her troubles. They stayed up for an hour in deep discussion, whispering in the dark so as not to wake up anyone in the house.

Mrs Clifford walked upstairs to the master bedroom with a broad grin on her face. Now she definitely had the upper hand. The little bitch would have to be terribly obedient and nice from now on so that she could earn what she seemed to hotly desire, a visit by that librarian.

"Well, you look happy enough." Mr Clifford glanced at his wife.

"Life is full of surprises." She blew him a kiss. "Wait and see." She had been unable to enlist the support of Mrs Ackroyd against the girl, but she would make life so miserable for her that she would resign on her own volition.

The following afternoon Mairi cycled down to the town centre to borrow another book, but above all to see Tristan. Arriving at the library, she saw him in a lively discussion with two attractive blonde women and she was stung by jealousy. But she quickly shook off that feeling because it was his job to talk to visitors and discuss book choices with them, regardless of whether they were good-looking women or not.

"Hi Mairi, how are you?" Tristan came over and gave her a hug.

"Could be better. And you Tristan?"

"Oh, I am just fine, but you don't look well. What is the matter?"

"It's about Mrs Clifford." Suddenly tears welled up in her eyes and all the thoughts about her work situation and the horrid mistress were laid bare to Tristan. "And she won't even let me have you over for tea."

Tears streamed down Mairi's cheeks. She wanted another hug from him, but he took a step back, shocked by the sudden explosion of bitter emotions.

"I am sorry to hear that, but please pull yourself together, Mairi. I can't have you creating a scene in my work place."

"So you don't want to listen to my worries?" She looked lost. "Tristan, don't you care about my well-being? Don't you understand? That cow is evil, she is hounding me no end, wants to have me fired!"

"Of course I do understand your concern. Don't be silly. But maybe you're overreacting and this is at any rate the wrong time for us to discuss your problems with Mrs Clifford. Look, people are coming through the door and I must welcome them. Let's talk tomorrow after work, all right?"

"It's not all right!" Mairi ran out the door and cycled up the hill again. She was in an emotional turmoil. She stopped and climbed off the bicycle by the roadside and sat down in the ditch and cried with her face in her hands.

Dinner was served without any complications although everyone could see that the house parlourmaid was tense yet she soldiered on and did her work to perfection.

"What's the matter with you?" Amanda peered at Mairi with concern in the kitchen.

"Don't want to talk about it." Mairi looked stubborn and it was to Amanda as if she had a protective shield around her, perhaps afraid to get hurt by Madam again.

CHAPTER SEVEN

Mr Clifford, smoking his pipe as usual, sat in the study with his wife on a Friday morning after breakfast. "I'm leaving ten pounds in this drawer for you to pay monthly bills today. I would normally do it myself as you know, but I am pretty busy with all these meetings this morning."

Mrs Clifford touched his shoulder. "Yes darling, no problem. I will see to it and get Mrs Ackroyd to post the letters with the money."

"What's the matter with Mairi by the way?" Mr Clifford glanced at his wife. "She seems so reticent all of a sudden."

Mrs Clifford shrugged. "Well, I don't know what's eating her. She is a trouble-maker anyway so God knows what she's been up to. I might ask Mrs Ackroyd."

"Yes please do." Mr Clifford nodded in appreciation. "Maybe she's homesick or something. She's so far away from her family you know. Maybe we should encourage her to write home more."

"I wouldn't worry about that lass." She snorted. "I'd be more than happy to send her on her way back to Scotland, if only to cure her homesickness."

Heading out the door, Mr Clifford felt a sting of guilt about the way he had been watching the girl move around his study when she vacuumed the floor the other day. Maybe she had noticed his gaze and felt uncomfortable. She did have a nice figure, and that pretty face, goodness. He promised himself to show more restraint when he had been drinking cognac.

The morning lapsed without anything noteworthy to tell what with Sarah doing her sewing before taking over the care of the boys when Mrs Clifford moved on to other things in her day. Mairi, still tight-lipped, made the beds, cleaned the floors, dusted off shelves and window sills where necessary and assisted Mrs Ackroyd who at noon was starting to make preparations for luncheon, which would be steak and kidney pie with mashed potatoes, beans and cabbage. Mrs Clifford was a stickler for vegetables because she believed they were good for her beloved children, and her husband too. He came home as usual for a quick bite.

But after luncheon, when her husband had driven back to the office, things started to go wrong. Mrs Clifford had sat down at her husband's desk to inspect the bills and, subsequently, counted the money in the drawer. Startled, she counted the notes twice. It wasn't difficult to remember what had happened in the morning. She had seen her husband place ten one-pound notes in the drawer, now there were only nine. Ergo, one pound was missing. She couldn't help but suspect Mairi of having stolen the money. Didn't that little minx who was so obviously after her husband try to steal a book in his study just a few weeks ago? Could she also be acting out as she hadn't been allowed to bring her librarian friend round? Mrs Clifford contemplated these incriminating facts. She realised she now had her opportunity to rid herself of that Scottish girl, once and for all. And next time they hired a house parlourmaid, she would make sure that they choose a middle-aged frump to deprive her impressionable husband of the chance to rob the cradle again.

Mrs Clifford swept into the kitchen, where Amanda and Mairi, clearing up, were startled by her abrupt appearance. "Girls. There is a pound note missing from my husband's study. Someone must have stolen it. I don't suspect Sarah, but one of you must have taken it. The guilty person better return the stolen money by tea time or I shall call the police. I won't stand for thieving under my roof!"

The mistress left the kitchen. Amanda and Mairi looked at each other. "What was that all about?" Amanda shrugged. Mairi stared at the floor. "Maybe she has made an excuse to get at me. I told you I saw her evil eye. I need to find out."

Mairi ran after Mrs Clifford into the hall and caught up with her in the dining room. A minute later she came back in tears and Amanda hugged her. "What's the matter dear?"

"I haven't stolen anything. I cannae give back money I haven't got. A pound is twice my weekly wages."

Mairi ran upstairs into the room she shared with Sarah and wrote letters to her father and Tristan. Everything in her mind was a blur and she knew that all this had to stop. As she wrote the letters she calmed down and became determined the way someone is who sees a solution at long last. She subsequently ventured downstairs again and into the kitchen. She eyed her friend with a sense of utter resignation, one of doom that worried Amanda.

"My dear Amanda, I enjoyed my time with you, but it's time for me to leave. Never ever shall I be accused of theft again. Forget about me, never think of me."

Amanda was so taken aback that Mairi was already out of the kitchen and through the back door before she had a chance to even reply, let alone persuade her to stay. Mairi rushed to the post office and then walked with relentless resolve in her step to a destination only she knew.

Amanda had a terrible gut feeling and made her way to the master's study where Mrs Clifford was writing letters. "Madam, Mairi has left us. Your accusation must have upset her."

Mrs Clifford looked up from her writing. "She's left us? Did she return the missing money? If not, this clearly shows she absconded as the thief she was. I wouldn't worry too much about her. Anyway, I want you to take these letters to the post office. It is important."

Amanda winced. "Yes, I will, but she has left without her bag, without her belongings. I'm worried about what she's up to. She said she had not stolen anything."

Mr Clifford came in the door, having returned from work early because of it being Friday. "What's going on? Who stole what?"

Mrs Clifford rose and hugged her husband. "Not to worry darling. I found a one-pound note missing from your drawer and I asked the girls if one of them had taken it with the result that Mairi has absconded. I told you she was no good and now we don't have to worry about sacking her. It seems she sacked herself."

Mr Clifford gave his wife an incredulous look. "Nothing was stolen for God's sake! I took the pound note out of the drawer because I realised you wouldn't need all that money to pay the bills. That's what's what. Mrs Ackroyd, please leave us. My wife and I need to discuss this in private."

Amanda was back in the kitchen on her own, worried sick about Mairi. They had only worked together for a month but she thought she knew her friend well, vulnerable, cagey at times, but also a sweet, witty girl, Madame Poirot eh?

Sarah joined her. "What was this accusation about?"

Amanda explained. "I didn't hear it, but it appears to me that Mrs Clifford later accused Mairi directly. If I had been her I would have invited Madam to search my room for the missing pound note, knowing I hadn't been out of the house. Mairi can't have been thinking straight or she wouldn't have gone away."

The following Saturday afternoon the postmaster, a middle-aged man with thinning hair, knocked on the door at Mr Craig's terraced home in the Lanarkshire village and presented him with a telegram from the police in Torquay.

"Something about next of kin," he said helpfully.

Mr Craig, who had just come home from the coal mine and was cleaning his lunch box, gave the sheet of paper a wary look. He finally accepted the telegram from the postman, handling it like an undetonated grenade. Sitting down to read the telegram, his face started to turn ashen, and the coal miner let out a howl filled with sorrow, alarming Brenda who came running to see what was going on. She read the lines too, sat down and buried her face in her hands.

"I'll catch the railway train to Torquay on Monday," he said after regaining his composure. "Just need to tell the manager I'm off for family reasons. The inquest I understand is on Tuesday morning."

On Monday morning, just as Mr Craig was about to leave for the train station, the postmaster came hurrying to his home with a letter written care of the Post Office. He recognised the handwriting and his grief grew deeper than he had thought possible.

Windsor Court was reeling with shock from the news that Mairi Craig had thrown herself to her death at Bishop's Walk. The police had knocked on the door at one o'clock in the afternoon on the day after the girl had left the house. Mr Clifford, who had just come home from the sail boat, had to go to the morgue to identify the deceased house parlourmaid.

"What did she look like?" Mrs Clifford eyed her husband as he entered the hall.

"I really don't want to talk about it." He walked straight to the bar. "I need a stiff whisky."

Amanda blamed herself for having taken Mairi to Bishop's Walk in the first place. "She was terrified by that steep drop and in some weird way she must have been drawn to it," she suggested to Sarah, who explained that she had a late-night talk with Mairi in the week before the accusation about theft had been made and where the girl had sounded truly depressed.

"Oh dear!" Amanda exclaimed. "We have to go to Sunday service tomorrow and the vicar, I'm sure, will say a few words about Mairi. I'm not sure I can take it. I miss her so badly. She was like a little sister to me, she was, you know."

Everyone in Windsor Court, except the children who had been taken care of elsewhere, went to church that Sunday morning; Mrs Clifford in shock aided by her husband as she stumbled down the road, with Amanda and Sarah following them, in tears.

After the initial singing of a hymn, the vicar addressed his little flock. "I noticed Mairi a few times as a church goer. She had lovely curly hair and I felt she listened to my sermons with sincerity."

He paused to observe the congregation, noticing that Mrs Ackroyd and Sarah had tears streaming down their cheeks. They snivelled, but tried to be quiet, a fact for which he was grateful. This sermon was difficult enough. The Cliffords stared into the distance, seemingly unable to fathom the situation, the utter tragedy that had befallen upon their home.

"I must now address the painful question of suicide. The Lord giveth and the Lord taketh. It is not for us to take our lives. It is a sin to commit suicide and anyone who does commit that sin cannot be buried in sacred ground."

Parts of the congregation gasped in disbelief. "This is not right!" Amanda cried out loud.

The vicar admonished her. "Please calm yourselves dear. This is a church. Respect the dignity of the church."

Sarah, shaking her head, took Amanda by the hand and escorted her out the door.

The Cliffords sat in the study and contemplated what was going to happen next. They had been informed that the inquest in St Marychurch was coming up on the following Tuesday and questions would be asked, but for the moment their minds were on writing an advert in the paper for a new house parlourmaid.

"Maybe we should wait a while." Mrs Clifford was worried that the expected newspaper headlines would put people off seeking work in a house of death. Journalists from papers as far as London, even Yorkshire and Scotland, had rang Windsor Court seeking more information after the police had issued their press release. Mr Clifford had instructed the maids they would make no comment.

"We'll offer good wages. Everyone has a price." Mr Clifford said.

Mrs Clifford agreed, but gave him a stern look. "The next maid we hire must be middle-aged, just like Sarah. Because of your penchant for young women, we've been going from one disaster after the other first with Abigail and then this Mairi." She spat out this last name as if it were contaminated.

Mr Clifford rose in anger. "I think I can control myself, Edith, but don't you try to put any blame for the suicide of this Scottish girl on me. The blame is squarely yours and never forget it. You need to change your ways around servants."

Mrs Clifford burst into tears. "But how could I have predicted that the stupid girl would go and throw herself to her death just because I suspected her of stealing that pound note? She must have had some death wish that nobody had detected. I also heard from Mrs Ackroyd that she had troubles with her mother. The girl obviously wasn't quite right in the head and she had problems with female authority. What a queer thing to do, killing herself like that."

"But why were you so quick to blame her?" He put his hands on her shoulders and stared her in the eye. "You could have waited until I came home and explained what had happened. But you had an axe to grind, didn't you! It's still all about Abigail, isn't it?"

Mrs Clifford fidgeted. "You know how humiliated I felt at the time, but now my worry is that the coroner will somehow accuse me of causing the death of that Scottish girl. I didn't accuse her directly!"

Mr Clifford took his wife in a gentle embrace. "I understand darling. There are so many aspects to this tragedy and it's certainly not all your fault, but you must be more careful in your dealings with servants from now on."

Seeking to appease her, he said he would take her advice on what sort of woman they hired next.

CHAPTER EIGHT

People gathered at the inquest in St Marychurch town hall on the Tuesday after Mairi's suicide. Among the attendants were the Cliffords, Mrs Ackroyd, Sarah, Mr Craig, Mr Williams the librarian and a gaggle of journalists from newspapers as far away as London. This upper class-lower class drama was news. The Cliffords sought out Mairi's father in the waiting room, offering their condolences on the death of his daughter. He gave Mrs Clifford a cold stare. She looked as if she was about to enter a tiger cage.

The coroner, Mr Johnson, invited a policeman to give testimony. He testified that the body of Mairi had been found on the preceding Saturday morning by two boys accompanied by a dog, the creature being the one that had discovered the body. The deceased must have walked up Bishop's Walk at Anstey's Cove on Friday afternoon and jumped to her death 150 feet down onto the cliffs on the water's edge. The forensic report showed she had suffered lacerations, a dislocated spine, a fractured skull and a broken neck, the last injury being the immediate cause of death.

The policeman continued: "Her injuries were severe and the position of the body was difficult, which meant it took five hours for the rescuers to bring it up from the cliffs by the waterfront to the foot path on Bishop's Walk. It's a steep drop, practically vertical. She must have hit the cliffs head-on with great velocity, at more than sixty miles an hour in fact and she fell 150 feet in just under four seconds based on gravitational estimates we've made.

"Her nose was crushed as well."

Everyone in the room gasped. "At least it was quick," Amanda whispered to Sarah.

"But you could tell she had been a pretty girl," the officer added, looking up from his report.

The coroner gave the policeman a curt glance. "That will be all thanks."

Sarah asked for permission to speak. "I spoke at length with Mairi one evening last week and she was in tears over her treatment by Mrs Clifford, who can be overly demanding if you don't mind me saying so."

She cast a shy look at Mrs Clifford who ignored her, seemingly locked in her own thoughts.

"She also felt down on her luck and depressed in general. I was worried about her, but didn't think she was that bad off."

Mr Clifford raised his hand. "Mairi could be shy and reticent at times, but I never noticed any serious problems with her. In fact, she was a delight to have as house parlourmaid. She will be sorely missed." He gave his wife a meaningful look.

The coroner heard evidence from Mrs Ackroyd that Mrs Clifford had entered the kitchen and accused the servants of stealing a pound note. "Somebody in the house must have taken it," Mrs Clifford had said. "If it is not returned by tea time I shall report it to the police."

Mrs Clifford, in evidence, said they had had a lot of trouble in the house lately, but that she did not specifically suspect that Mairi had taken the money. But, the inquest heard, the girl had remained upset and refused to eat. She had gone to her room upstairs apparently to sulk for a while and then came to the kitchen door and said goodbye.

"I did not see her again," the cook witnessed.

In reply to the coroner, Mrs Clifford said she regretted having made the remark. "Of course I am sorry I said what I said, but I seriously thought someone had stolen money."

"Did you put it to her more severely than Mrs Ackroyd?" The coroner eyed her.

"No."

"It is a grave matter to accuse someone of stealing." He uttered the words with a serious air of consideration.

"I did not accuse anyone." Mrs Clifford spoke in her deep voice with a defiant tone, but everyone in the room could see that she was uncomfortable. She kept clutching her pearl necklace as if her nerves were on end.

At this point Mr Craig rose in anger and presented the coroner with the last letter his daughter had written to him before throwing herself to her death. She had posted it in Wellswood before going up Bishop's Walk where she perished. He had brought the letter with him from Lanarkshire.

"I had thought my most precious daughter was happy in her situation here, but this her last letter to me tells a different story." He gave Mrs Clifford a grim stare.

He handed the letter to the coroner who started to read it: "Dear Dad, many thanks for your letter. Hope you are fine, and had a good time over the holidays. Don't let this letter cause you any anxiety, only, you see, Mrs Clifford has refused to let me invite a nice young man I met to Windsor Court, but she allows Amanda to have her boyfriend over. Now this afternoon Mrs Clifford accused me of stealing a pound note, and deliberately told me that I had done it.

She never liked me you see, just like ma. Well, old man, I am just about fed up. I'm down here doing my best. This is the second time I've been accused of stealing after ma accused me at home if you remember. It will be my last. I am innocent, but life isn't fair. By the time you see this I shall be gone for ever. Dad, beloved, this is the only way out. You know I love you. Don't worry, best of luck, your ever loving daughter. Mairi."

People in the audience flinched, some sobbed.

Tristan Williams rose, pale-faced, and said he had also received a last letter from Mairi. He handed it to the coroner, who read it too.

"Dear Tristan, my prince. Please forgive me for taking my life, but above all forget me. I was going to buy a new coat, but I won't need it now. Life isn't for weak ones like me. Please tell everyone to forget me. I'm a failure as I am sure you realised when I came to you crying at the library. I'm sorry for creating a scene."

Mairi had spoken twice from the other side, from her grave, wherever it was.

"In the face of these letters," said the coroner, summing up, "I have no doubt in my own mind that the house parlourmaid had intended to commit suicide consequent on her being accused of stealing. There may also have been a degree of depression that aggravated the whole situation, given that Mrs Clifford seems to have treated the girl unfairly. But it is a matter of profound regret that Mrs Clifford used those words, and only shows how very careful one must be in accusing people before it is proven that a crime has been committed. Everyone is innocent until proven guilty.

"Mrs Clifford," he turned to her again with a stern look. "No crime has been committed. But you will have to live for the rest of your life with a sense of guilt for the self-inflicted death of a fine young woman."

He returned a verdict of suicide while of an "unsound mind". The verdict was reported by newspapers all over England. Even The

Times of London and newspapers as north as Scotland told the story about the unhappy maid.

Back at Windsor Court, everyone settled in for lunch although nobody showed much appetite. Mrs Ackroyd did the cooking and Sarah served the food in the dining room. The little boys were blissfully unaware of the drama, another nurse having been asked to look after them the whole day at a nearby farm.

Mr Clifford, as distressed as everyone else in Windsor Court, tried to make sense of the situation as he and his wife, Mrs Ackroyd and Sarah retreated to the living room for coffee and cognac, which they normally never had with servants but this was not a normal occasion.

"So what happens now?" He glanced at the two remaining servants. "I have noticed that both of you are unhappy with the situation following the unfortunate demise of poor Mairi. I can fully understand it if you want to leave us, but jobs are scarce and you should consider that too. My wife and I would like you to stay."

He turned to his wife for support, but her mind appeared to be vacant.

Silence prevailed for a moment until Sarah spoke. "I am happy to stay, Sir. I don't see myself finding a man and getting married at my age, and I do adore the little boys. I want to be there for them. If you don't mind."

Mr Clifford nodded. "Sarah, we are most grateful for your continued commitment. We value your services and our sons love you. I'll make it up for you, no doubt, in terms of remuneration."

Mrs Clifford remained lost in thought and seemed incapable of following the discussion. Her husband glanced at her but continued nonetheless. "Mrs Ackroyd? What about you please? You've been with us for something like four years and we enjoy your cooking as always and respect your integrity and commitment to your duties. What is your pleasure?"

Amanda thought long and hard. This was a good job, well-paid, good outings and she had earned the respect of her employers, which probably was more important than everything else; the sense of job continuity. She wasn't going to be sacked in a hurry. But then she considered the fate of Mairi and she also wanted a new start in life, marry Steve. Maybe this was the trigger.

She looked Mr Clifford straight in the eye, ignoring Mrs Clifford. "Sir, there is a dark shadow resting on this house, the dark shadow of Mairi, my friend and colleague. She wasn't buried in a cemetery and it bothers me. I'll hand in my resignation if you don't mind, Sir. I shan't work here anymore, but thanks for these years, Sir. Thanks for having me."

Mrs Clifford suddenly broke into a hysterical laughter that startled and frightened everyone in the room. Had she gone mad?

She rose and walked up to Amanda.

"Mrs Ackroyd, do you see her in the night as well? "

The lady of the house collapsed on the floor in tears.

EPILOGUE

The advertisement in the Western Morning News read: "Wanted as soon as possible, two Ladies, COOK and HOUSE PARLOURMAID, to help NURSE run house. Good outings. Apply by letter, stating salary required. Windsor Court, Torquay."

The Cliffords ended up hiring a middle-aged woman as house parlourmaid and an elderly lady as a cook. Sarah had found her own weekly wages doubled. Mr Clifford had told her that she would be the most senior servant from now on, earning more than any newcomer, including the cook. Loyalty was rewarded, he had reassured her. It had warmed her heart to feel appreciated, although she would never forget the fate of Mairi, the bubbly, sometimes sad parlourmaid with that quirky accent.

Sarah kept in touch with Amanda who was keen to know what went on in the house that had been her home for four years. The former cook at Windsor Court had sought a lodging near to her boyfriend in Paignton and she was planning to move in with him once they married in their local church in the presence of families and friends. She would never visit the church in Wellswood again.

Mrs Clifford, whose bad conscience left her no rest, was frequently terrified by sounds and visions in the night to the point where she would stay with her sister most of the time except on holidays such as Christmas and Easter. They sold the house two years later and moved to Totnes to the west, beyond Paignton. Mr Clifford, having made good at last in the services, went on to become a celebrated commander in the Royal Navy in the Second World War while Mrs Clifford engaged in charity.

In 1943, on the 10th anniversary of Mairi's suicide, they invested £25,000 in a charity providing education to young women in service with the purpose of improving their career opportunities, giving them a better chance to succeed in life. They did so after consulting Mrs Ackroyd and Sarah. The charity was named the Mairi Craig Trust.

ABOUT THE AUTHOR

Rolf Söderlind, a Swedish national, is a retired foreign correspondent who reported world news from twenty countries on four continents for Reuters, the Associated Press and United Press International. He is now a resident of Torquay where he stumbled on the fate of the vulnerable parlourmaid while researching the history of the hundred-year-old stone house where he lives with his wife, Heather.

Life in Torquay is not the same anymore for Rolf. The house has taken on a new dimension. "I cook in the kitchen where the house parlourmaid was wrongly accused of theft, I eat in the dining room where she once served the owners and their guests, and I sit down for a moment of contemplation in the bedroom where I believe she wrote her suicide letter. I have read it. I have read the news reports from the inquest. The rest is fiction."

ACKNOWLEDGEMENTS

In no particular order, I have been helped by Janet Laurence, an editor who on behalf of Writers' Workshop carried out an editorial assessment of my manuscript to ensure that it adheres to 1930s habits and language in England. John Norman, my brother-in-law, gave further feedback on the zeitgeist. Tora, my youngest daughter, provided input on feelings between women while Heather, my wife, has given overall advice. I must also mention John Tucker, Local & Family History Librarian at the Torquay Library, who helped me to a crucial newspaper clipping about the tragedy that I couldn't find in the digitised records of the British Library. Last and not least: I beg forgiveness of those whose names I have failed to mention.

Lightning Source UK Ltd.
Milton Keynes UK
UKHW04f0836230818
327682UK00011B/324/P